# You are Enough

Written by Graham Arnold

Illustrated by Jen Holcombe

Dottie was ever so excited,
today would be the day,
she was going to see her Daddy,
who so long had been away.

She woke up in a hurry,
and put her best dress on,
it was ever so important,
not to get the dress code wrong.

She didn't eat much breakfast,
afraid to drop a crumb,
she had to look her best for Daddy,
even though she was so young.

As she left the house for Daddy,
She gave her shoes a shine,
She knew that he would like it,
And it was worth the time.

Walking down the garden,
She saw a lovely rose,
She picked it for her Daddy,
And smelt it with her nose.

Further on the apple tree,
With apples oh so bright,
Her Daddy would love one of them,
He'd light up with delight.

She knew it wasn't long now,
And she hoped that he'd remember,
The good times that they'd had,
When they were last together.

She turned the final corner,
And gave herself a fright,
Looking in the window,
She saw she was a sight.

Weeping uncontrollably,
She couldn't face her Dad,
Her dress, her tights, her hair, her
look, just made her very sad!

When her Daddy saw her there,
His heart was sadly broken,
He lifted her and cuddled her,
And said something softly
spoken.

"You are enough, just as you are." His face lit up and smiled. "You are enough, just as you are. My heart, my love, my child."

Heavenly Father,
Thankyou that I am
enough,
Thankyou that you love
me just as I am.
Amen.

Printed in Great Britain
by Amazon